There Is a Bird on Your Head!

To Lee and Diane

ISBN-13: 978-0-545-11598-8
ISBN-10: 0-545-11598-1

36 35   17/0

Printed in the U.S.A.   40

First Scholastic printing, January 2009

There Is a Bird on Your Head!

By **Mo Willems**

An **ELEPHANT & PIGGIE** Book

SCHOLASTIC INC.

New York   Toronto   London   Auckland   Sydney
Mexico City   New Delhi   Hong Kong   Buenos Aires

Is something on my head?

Yes.

8

There is a bird
on my head?

aggghhh!!!

Is there a
bird on my
head now?

No.

Now there are two
birds on your head.

16

They are
in love!

17

They are love birds!

19

How do you
know they are
love birds?

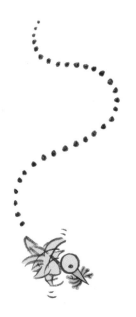

Two birds are making a nest on my head?

24

I am afraid to ask . . .

Then I have good news!

Now, I have three baby chicks on my head!

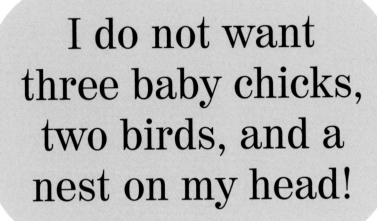

I do not want three baby chicks, two birds, and a nest on my head!

Where do you want them?

48

Okay.
I will try asking.

51

53

You are welcome. . . .

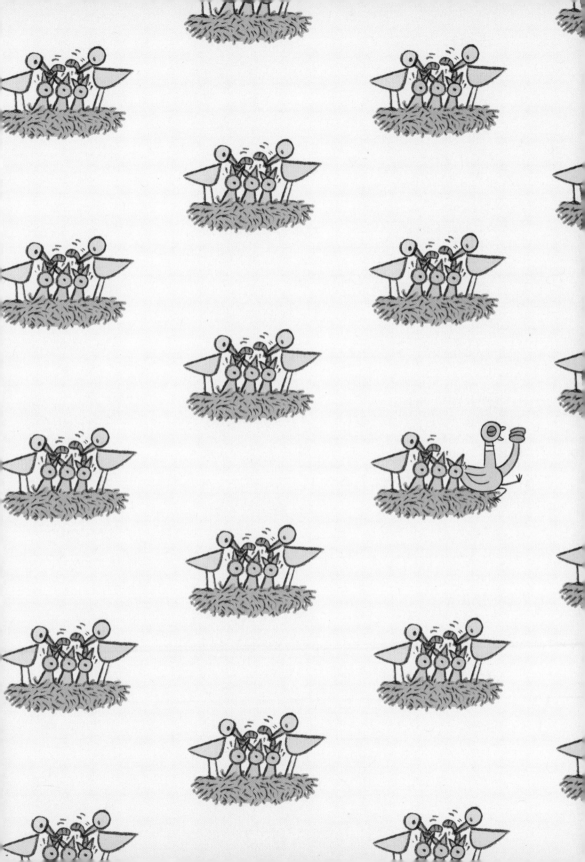